THINGS ELLIE LIKES

OTHER BOOKS ABOUT ELLIE AND TOM

What's Happening to Ellie?
A book about puberty for girls and young
women with autism and related conditions
ISBN 978 1 84905 526 0
eISBN 978 0 85700 937 1

Ellie Needs to Go
A book about how to use public toilets
safely for girls and young women with
autism and related conditions
ISBN 978 1 84905 524 6
eIBSN 978 0 85700 938 8

What's Happening to Tom?
A book about puberty for boys and young
men with autism and related conditions
ISBN 978 1 84905 523 9
eISBN 978 0 85700 934 0

Things Tom Likes
A book about sexuality and masturbation for boys
and young men with autism and related conditions
ISBN 978 1 84905 522 2
eISBN 978 0 85700 933 3

Tom Needs to Go
A book about how to use public toilets
safely for boys and young men with
autism and related conditions
ISBN 978 1 84905 521 5
eISBN 978 0 85700 935 7

BY THE SAME AUTHOR

Sexuality and Severe Autism
A Practical Guide for Parents,
Caregivers and Health Educators
ISBN 978 1 84905 327 3
eISBN 978 0 85700 666 0

THINGS ELLIE LIKES

A book about sexuality and masturbation for girls and young women with autism and related conditions

KATE E. REYNOLDS

Illustrated by Jonathon Powell

Jessica Kingsley *Publishers*
London and Philadelphia

First published in 2015
by Jessica Kingsley Publishers
73 Collier Street
London N1 9BE, UK
and
400 Market Street, Suite 400
Philadelphia, PA 19106, USA

www.jkp.com

Copyright © Kate E. Reynolds 2015
Illustration copyright © Jonathan Powell 2015

Library of Congress Cataloging in Publication Data
A CIP catalog record for this book is available from the Library of Congress

British Library Cataloguing in Publication Data
A CIP catalogue record for this book is available from the British Library

ISBN 978 1 84905 525 3
eIBSN 978 0 85700 936 4

Printed and bound in China

With thanks to Kate Hope, Irene Buckley, Cherry Miller, Rachael Bolitho, Debbie Coles and Kerry Sant, clinical nurse specialists at the Royal United Hospital, Bath.

Thanks also to my friends Cathy Roberts, Carrie Fyall, Vinny Ringrose, Sarah Davies, Sharon Butler, Angela Gabriel and Anne Callahan for their support.

Kate

Thanks to my father, Bernard Powell, for all the encouragement and help through the years.

Jonathon

A NOTE FOR PARENTS AND CAREGIVERS

One of the most important lessons for a person with autism to learn is the difference between 'public' and 'private'. Often concepts are hard to explain, so this story takes the reader through some of Ellie's experiences to give young women with autism solid examples of public and private behaviours. In addition, the story outlines public and private zones of the bodies of both young women and young men.

The book shows explicit images of Ellie masturbating and explains how this is a private sexual behaviour that she should only do when she is alone in her bedroom. Masturbation is presented as one of many pleasurable things for Ellie and highlighted as a natural activity that is enjoyed by typically developing girls and young women and those with autism.

This is Ellie. Ellie likes dancing. She can do this anywhere – at home, or outside where there are other people. Lots of other people like dancing, too.

Ellie likes making pizza and listening to music. Lots of other people like doing this, too.

Ellie also likes touching her vagina and clitoris, which is the tiny lump near the hole which is her vagina. Her clitoris and vagina are protected by her vulva, which is the fleshy skin at the front between her legs.

Lots of other girls and women like touching their vaginas and clitorises, too. This is called masturbation.

Ellie knows some things are PRIVATE. This means that no one else listens to, watches or can walk in and see what Ellie is doing. Ellie is alone. This means she only does private things in her own bedroom.

Ellie knows some things are PUBLIC.
This means that other people can
see and hear what Ellie is doing.

Ellie does not touch her vagina, clitoris or breasts when she is in public.

Ellie also has private zones on her body. These are her clitoris, vulva, vagina, buttocks and breasts. This is the same for all girls and women. Ellie knows the rule that private zones are hidden by underwear. For girls and women this means underpants and bras.

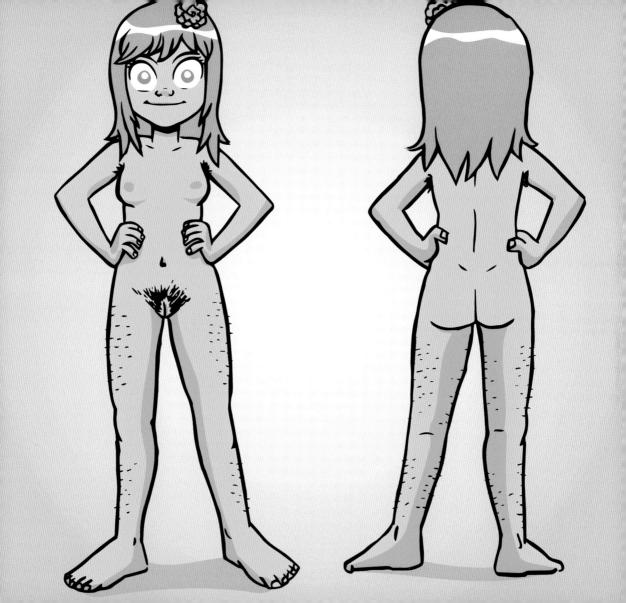

Ellie knows that boys and men also have private zones of their bodies. These are their testicles, penises and buttocks.

Ellie knows that in public, everyone hides their private zones with clothes. No one touches anyone else's private zones in public, not even through clothes.

Sometimes Ellie feels excited and wants to touch her clitoris, vagina and breasts when she is in a public place. But she knows she must wait until she gets home.

Ellie closes her bedroom door. Then she undoes her bra and underpants and touches her breasts and her vagina and clitoris. Touching her breasts and vagina and clitoris is a private thing that Ellie enjoys doing. Ellie knows she must only do this when she is alone in her bedroom, like other girls.

Although Ellie's vagina is usually wet, it can get really wet when she is very excited. She knows to wipe it with tissue and put the tissue in the bin.

Ellie puts on any clothes she has taken off and then washes her hands.

Ellie feels happy and relaxed now. She goes back downstairs to join her family watching television. Great, it's her favourite DVD!

ABOUT THE SERIES

Sexuality and sexual safety are often difficult subjects for parents, caregivers and health educators to broach with young people who have severe forms of autism and related conditions. These young people are widely perceived as being 'vulnerable', but the lack of sex education and social opportunities available only increases that vulnerability, leaving them open to child sex and other abuse. Unlike typically developing children who learn by 'osmosis' from their peers, our young people need clear and detailed information provided by those who support them.

This is one of a series of six books – three for girls and young women and three addressing issues for boys and young men. Each book tells a story about the key characters, Ellie and Tom, giving those supporting young women and men something tangible as a basis for further questions from young people. The wording is unambiguous and avoids euphemisms that may confuse readers and listeners. Many young people with severe forms of autism and related conditions are highly visual, so the illustrations are explicit and convey the entire story.

These books are designed to be read with a young person with autism, alongside other more generic reading material.